Dog Days

Devil's Land Stories

Terry Hooker

Published by Blue Dahlia Publishing House, 2023.

Table of Contents

This story is dedicated to Miss Annie, the blessed soul
who saved the real Buddy.

Chapter 1
The Poor Beast

"Fucking cows!" Jo muttered under her breath as she tore the last of the branches off the heifer so she could get back to the barn. She had noticed one heifer missing from the herd as they came in to get food. She was pretty sure this one was bred, so Jo wanted to make sure she hadn't given birth somewhere. The rain had started earlier in the day, but with all the other ranch chores, Jo hadn't thought too much about the wet weather until the thunder started rolling in. The rain was coming down in literal sheets as she tugged the last branch away. The cow took off, spraying Jo with what she hoped was just mud in its effort to get back to the herd. Jo quickly mounted her mare, a good old girl who had stood patiently as the rain pelted her.

"c'mon girl, let's make sure she can find her way back. We don't have to go searching again." She used the reins to turn the horse around, even though the mare was an old hack at this and moved with just the slightest shift in Jo's body, she wanted to hurry home to her warm shower and cozy bed.

The rain poured off the edges of her old Stetson; she wore her dad's old cowboy raincoat with its split sides, so her legs stayed relatively dry as she rode home. With rain such as this, though, no amount of rain gear could keep her totally dry.

Thunder rolled in the background; the flash of lightning lit the sky as bright as noon. In the corner of her eye, she saw a small furry thing lying in the mud. She tried to ignore it and urged the mare forward, trying to keep the heifer in her sight. Then, in that one moment of quiet before the next crash of thunder rolled over the prairie, she heard a small whimper.

Jo sighed, damned her soft heart, and turned to see what poor beast was drowning in the rain in mud out in her cattle fields.

She pulled the mare up short and hopped down; no need to step on the poor beast because it was dark, and she couldn't see quite clearly. She reached in her saddle bags, grateful her father had always told her to keep them "packed up for emergencies, no tellin' what you might need out in the dark and the rain."

Jo smiled at the memory; her dad was always one to be prepared. Or so she had thought.

As she reached the animal, she dropped to her knees and saw it was a small dog. A terrier-type from what she could tell. No color was discernible with all the rain and mud, but it was clear that he was terribly hurt.

"C'mon, boy, this isn't going to feel good, but at least if you die, you won't die alone." She scooped him up, surprised at how small his frame was. He must have been out for a while; he was so bony she knew the ride home wasn't going to be comfortable for her either. She threw him over the mares back in front of the saddle and swung up herself. She opened her raincoat and gently tucked him inside, then urged the mare forward toward the warmth of the house.

She carried the dog into the house, gently laying him on the old washing machine while she slipped off her boots and hung up her coat and hat to dry. The rest of her clothes would need to be changed soon, and a hot shower was in her future, but right now, this little guy needed her attention.

She found a towel still in the dryer, wrapped the mud-covered pup back up, and carried him to the fire. The fireplace was enormous! Big enough to heat most of the house at one time. Jo loved sleeping on the couch in front of the fire, so she rarely turned the heat on. With just her in the large home, there didn't seem to be a need to.

"Okay, buddy, as much of a mess as you are, I think tonight will just be about getting you warm, and hopefully, you'll make it through to morning." The brown eyes watched her as she laid down pillows and blankets, then placed him gently on top, still wrapped in the towel.

Being a working rancher, Jo had a good idea of what to do to help the little guy feel better. She quickly changed her clothes into warm sweats, then grabbed some goat milk out of the freezer. Goat milk was best for wayward baby animals. She heated it up as fast as she dared and grabbed a large syringe, the kind with the plastic, not the needle, and stepped back into the living room.

The room was full of shadows as the flames licked the top of the fireplace. Jo was surprised that the fire was going so well, but didn't question too much. "At least something's going right tonight."

She gently uncovered the little dog, who had dried while waiting for her. She rubbed it gently with the towel, knocking off as much mud as she could. The little dog flinched through most of this. Jo could see the claw marks all over the little guy. "Oh buddy, what did you get yourself into?"

She slowly fed him the whole bowl of goat's milk until his stomach was full and he had curled up on his makeshift bed. Gently, he started to snore. Jo stood and stretched, patted the dog, covered him back up with a blanket, and cleaned up the remnants of her first aid work. It was close to three in the morning, and her body ached from the day. The shower she was dreaming about would have to wait. She grabbed her big fluffy blanket that her great grandmother June had hand-sewn and was snoring right along with the dog in no time at all.

Chapter 2
Buddy

The water in the tub was dark brown; Jo wasn't sure if it was from all the mud or all the dried blood coming off the poor little dog. He was such a good boy, standing perfectly still as she gently poured warm water over his body. Tremors shook his little body as she worked. She wasn't sure if it was from the cold, pain, or fear, but Jo did her best to comfort him.

"It's okay, buddy, no one will hurt you here. I got you." When she had rinsed as much as she had dared, Jo wrapped him back up in the biggest comfiest towel she could find. She carried him back into the kitchen, where the light was best, so she could assess his injuries.

Standing there, holding the little dog still on the kitchen table, Jo could see the claw marks ravaging his body. "Sheesh, buddy, did you stumble on a whole nest of cougars or what?" She could not believe that this little guy was still alive! She knew if he survived any infections that might be coming his way, he was definitely a fighter and would have a home wherever she landed.

Her equine first aid kit was closest to grab, so she cleaned each cut individually and sprayed them down with Al- U- Shield, a silver medicated spray that worked wonders on any cuts her horses received. By the time she finished the doctoring, the little dog was so covered in silver he looked like a bad replica of a robot. His tongue lolled out of his smiling face, and his tail beat a furious rhythm, letting Jo know he was feeling better. She warmed up some more goat's milk, mixed in some white rice she had cooked off, and made sure his tummy was warm and full. Buddy, as she had come to call the little guy, then did three turns under the table by her feet before laying down to snore the morning away.

Chapter 3

Between a Rock and a Slime ball

Jo held her head in her hands as she looked at the computer screen. She knew she could make it if that bastard would just let the will get out of escrow. She knew he was just holding it up to try to drive her out, make her sell to him. Or worse, sleep with him to save her house. She would never know how her dad had thought he was a good man. Of course, when this was first written up, it was the bastard's dad who ran the law firm. Kyle was nothing like his dad.

Mr. Brown had been sweet and kind. He had worked hard and pulled himself up by his bootstraps, where his son had been given everything he wanted. Except, of course, her and her land. She growled slightly at the thought of the slimy asshat. Her dad had died almost a year ago from a massive heart attack out in the field with his beloved cattle. She would never forget the fear of not being able to find him. She got on her mare and rode each path she thought he would have taken. On the way back, she had seen all the heifers in a circle out in the closest field. Her heart had dropped as she kicked the mare into a run. She threw herself off the horse before it had stopped; the momentum carried her through the herd to where her dad was lying peacefully in the green grass, a slight smile on his face. His eyes were still open as he stared at the deep blue sky, the line of sight only broken by his beloved cows.

Jo shook herself out of the thought. She didn't have time to feel sadness or regret. She had to find a way to keep the ranch. She loved the land as much as her dad had. She let out a sigh that sounded very similar to a growl at the same time that Buddy began to squirm and cry. She gently rubbed the dog with her stocking feet until he settled down.

"Can't have that now Buddy, don't want to pull any of those cuts open." The small dog growled slightly, then settled down on the foot that wasn't petting him. Jo smiled as he began to twitch and run in his sleep.

"We'll figure this out soon, Bud; you'll get to run free through the ranch soon."

Evening approached in a golden and pink hue; the cows lowed in the barn waiting for their nightly meal. The aroma of homemade marinara sauce wafted throughout the house. Jo tried to cook large meals a few times a week and eat on that for as long as she could. Today had been cooking day. She sat on the old bench by the back door and pulled on her boots. Her head was filled with all the chores she had to get done this evening. She didn't notice the little dog get up, stretch, and then pad over to sit beside her.

She scratched the little dog under his chin, "you must be feeling better, Buddy. Wanna come out to the barn with me? Keep me company from the night?"

Buddy's thick little tail thumped on the wooden floor. As she stood to go, so did he, a big smile on his face as he followed her through the yard to the barn. He stayed right by her as she worked through the chores, close enough to touch but never in the way. She kept on a running commentary about each cow, telling him how much they weighed, who their sire was, how much each ate, and anything else she could think of. Buddy stayed next to her, tilting his head in such a way as if he understood what she was talking about.

This was her happy place, wandering around with the cows, listening to the birds singing their evening song, the smell of the fresh hay that she had cut a few days ago. This was what the world should be. Buddy seemed to understand this and fit right into the equation. After the last of the chores were done and she had recorded the last entry into the care journal for the day, she turned to head back to the house. Her smile faded the moment she saw the cherry red Porsche 911 coming down her drive. She could not see the color in the fading sun but knew the car by the snake driving it.

Buddy whimpered slightly at her side; she reached down to check him to see if he was hurting from the trip to the barn. She squatted down next to him and examined every inch of his claw marks. They would need a fresh coat of Al-U-Shield, but nothing was open or oozing.

"What the Hell is that, Jo? Some sort of robot hybrid?" Even his voice annoyed her. Buddy growled low and deep, not loud enough for Kyle to hear it but enough for Jo to recognize the dog and man were not going to be friendly. She kept her hand on the little dog, as much for herself as to keep him in check. No need to have Kyle attacked on her property. He would find a way to use that to get what he wanted, or at least he would try.

Kyle circled them, watching like the predator he was. "Where did you find such a sad-looking dog? It is a dog, right?" He pulled out a pack of cigarettes and started to reach for his lighter.

"No smoking on the ranch, you know that." Jo stood up to her full five foot eleven height and ran her hands down her jeans, trying to dislodge some of the dirt and manure that had embedded itself in the fabric. These weren't her favorite pants, or she would have pulled on overalls over them.

"Really, Jo, still?"

"Yes, Kyle, just like it's been for decades now, no smoking. I don't want you starting a fire and killing my animals." This was said over her shoulder as she walked toward the house, hoping he would get the picture and hop back in his fancy car and leave. But that was not Kyle's style, nope. He chuckled, put the cigarette and lighter back in his pocket, and followed her to the back door.

With a sigh, she turned toward him as she ascended the last step, "Kyle, what do you want?"

"Can't an old friend just come by and check-in every once in a while?"

"No, Kyle, they can't. Especially not when that 'friend' is trying to run me off my land."

"Okay, okay. Jo, I was just worried about you. Out here all by yourself. I worry you'll be hurt." He had taken the last two steps up, so he was almost pressed against her. He lifted his hand and began to stroke her cheek. Jo had nowhere to go. She was pinned between the door and this slime of a human being. She thought about kneeing him in the groin but was trying not to antagonize him in any way. She really didn't want him mad at her. Who knows what kind of legal mumbo jumbo he would pull out then to get the ranch.

The step began to vibrate as Jo stood there glaring up at Kyle's smirk. A low rumbling could be heard as the stairs began to shake just enough to throw off the man's balance. Jo, being pinned to the door, held steady as Kyle crashed through the wooden rail and landed face first in the mud.

Jo stifled a laugh, quickly turning it into a throat clear. "Um, you okay?"

Kyle sputtered and spat out mud and muck as he got himself back into standing position. "Uh yeah. I think your stairs might be a little out of wack. Might want to fix them." He stood there, trying to wipe the mud off himself, but only succeeded in smearing it worse.

"There's a hose around front if you need to clean up. I need to check my dinner. It's in the crock pot. Have a good night, Kyle." Jo and Buddy scurried into the house, closing the door firmly behind them. Jo made sure the lock was secured before she crumbled to the ground, shaking with laughter and tears.

Chapter 4
Just a Girl

Buddy loved the ride into town in the big, old pickup truck. Jo hadn't been sure if the little dog would be frightened of it, but the minute she rolled the window down, he stuck his head out, tongue blowing in the wind. Jo had to laugh at how absolutely silly he looked, still covered in silver, deep slashes still marking his body, but the pure joy in his face let her know he was feeling okay. This made her let a breath out; they were headed to the vet to ensure all was good with the little dog.

She carried him in; he wasn't so big that he was a burden but still not too small as to be an easy carry. He happily sat on her lap in the office, smiling at all the office ladies as they all came by to tell him what a handsome boy he was. Jo was pretty sure he must have had a family at some point. There was no way he could be this well-behaved with strangers patting and loving all over him if he hadn't. He thought he was the king!

"Jo, you ready?" Dr. Matt was such a nice man, always with a smile on his face. He was chuckling at her now, knowing any animal that crossed her path was in for a great life.

"Let's see what you have here." Buddy turned straight toward the Doc, licking his beard. "Oh, hi Buddy, looks like Jo tried to turn you into a robot. Oh, what a good boy you are, such a good boy. Ha, ha, but you have to let me turn you around!" Dr. Matt laughed.

"Looks like you cleaned him up pretty well. Al-U-Shield was a good call there, Jo kept it all clean and started the healing process. Any idea what attacked him? I can't place these claw marks." His brow furrowed as he examined the little dog's injuries. "It almost looks like a bird claw, but there is no way there's a bird that big out there, and the strikes seem more like a large cat. Hmmm."

Shaking his head, Dr. Matt took out a magnifying glass and took a closer look at the long slices on the back of Buddy. He hummed and hawed before putting the glass down. "I have no idea what did this, but Jo, whatever it is, it's big. Any of the calves missing?"

"They are all fine; nothing is missing, not even the useless old barn cat."

"Well, you did a good job with him. If things don't work out, maybe you should consider a career as a vet or vet tech."

Jo smiled her best smile at him. The whole town knew what was going on. Even though they sympathized with her, many of the old-timers didn't think a girl should be running a ranch. She shook his hand and thanked him for taking such good care of her new boy. He waved off any fee saying she did most of the work; he was just there to consult. She cranked the truck and headed back to the ranch; other errands forgotten as tears streamed down her face. Maybe they were all right. Perhaps this was too much for her. A warm tongue gently licked her tears away. Buddy then lay across her lap as she drove, commiserating with her in her despair.

Chapter 5

Invasion

Jo could see at least six vehicles at her house as they drove down the long drive. She stepped on the gas and flew to a stop in the front drive, afraid there had been some sort of accident with the cattle and the neighbors were there to help while she had been gone. As she threw herself out of the truck, Kyle came around the corner with a group of men in business suits.

"And this is prime land for any type of development you would like, or you could keep it as a working ranch. The possibilities are endless, gentlemen." His smile was so sleazy; Jo was shocked oil wasn't rolling off him.

"What in the hell are you doing on my land?" she growled as she stomped over to the group. "Whatever this man is telling you is false! This is my land; it's not for sale. The bank doesn't own any part of it, and neither does Mr. Brown." Buddy had come along at her side; his hair was standing up on his back as he snarled at the group.

"Now, now Jo, as things look, you won't own the ranch more than a few months more, and I am trying to help you out here, get you a buyer, so you don't drown in financial ruin." He smiled at the group of men who were now moving around nervously. "Don't worry, gentlemen, with the right deal, Miss Seraph will make the move. I just know it."

"You don't know jack shit, you little turd." Her finger was waving under his nose, and spittle flew from her mouth as her anger and hurt cascaded out. "This land has been with my family for generations. If you think I'm going to sell or worse, let some slimy toad like you swindle it away from me, you haven't seen what Hell I can rain down on you!"

As she was yelling at Kyle, the other men had scurried to their cars and began to drive away. Jo noticed this from the corner of her eye as she clamped down on Kyle. "If you would be even one percent as decent as your father had been, none of this would be happening. The fact that you are holding all of this up makes you the worst of the worst. Not even a man. You are scum!" The last word echoed across the fields. The cows looked up from their grazing, though they took little interest in the goings-on at the house.

Chapter 6
The World Shook

The first slap landed with as much force as shock. Jo didn't see it coming. It knocked her to the ground where she looked up at Kyle, the anger rolling off him in waves matched only by her own rage.

"How dare you mess up my sale! You little bitch! If you think you are going to keep this land, you have no idea who you are messing with! This will be mine one way or another!" the last word echoed off the old house just as he began kicking her.

She felt the ground shake under her but was too busy trying to protect her soft areas while attempting to grab his foot. She succeeded in pulling off Kyle's shoe, but he continued to kick her in a blind rage. The ground echoed the growling sounds she thought were coming from Kyle until the blur went over her and landed on Kyle, knocking him at least twenty feet back.

"Buddy, NO!" She jumped to her feet to try to save the little dog who had sprung into action to keep her safe.

She slid to a stop feet from the melee to see her sweet, lovable little terrier had not only attacked with such force as to knock a grown man flat on the ground but to make the little dog look much bigger than he had been. The claw marks on his back were ripped open over bulging muscles, and his cute little snout was filled with vicious-looking teeth dripping with saliva. The tail she had felt just yesterday thumping on her foot now stood straight out like a sword.

The craziest part was the image of two other heads next to the one drooling on Kyle. It was like a mirage, fading in and out. Jo guessed Kyle must have hit her in the head harder than she thought. She shook herself.

"Get your dog off of me. I am going to sue you for this!"

Jo quietly called to Buddy, not sure he would answer. Still, he immediately stepped off Kyle, looking small and cute as he always had except for the blood around his mouth where he had bitten Kyle in the shoulder to hold him down. Buddy trotted over to Jo and sat obediently at her feet.

"I think if anyone is doing the suing, it will be me. I am going in to call the Sheriff now. I will be pressing charges. If you think my dog getting you off me as you tried to kill me is going to get you anywhere, stick around and talk to the Sheriff, we can let him sort it out."

As she turned to head back into the house, Buddy was right at her side. Her hands were shaking to much to pick up the phone, making her shake more with anger and bringing her to her to her knees crying as she hugged the little dog that had saved her life.

Chapter 7
Reality

"Jo, I really think you should go see the doctor. I'm worried about those ribs." The Sheriff himself had come out; he did not send a deputy for this mess. Jo found that somewhat ironic. It took her getting the crap kicked out of her for anyone to come to her aid. Okay, she wasn't totally being fair. Most people here tried to mind their own business, but come on! A little help while she had been getting financially beaten up would have been nice. It took actual beating up for someone to step in and stop it.

"I think you should file a restraining order; I sent my guys to pick him up, but I can't guarantee that any charges will be placed. If it was up to me, it would be. It's a good thing you have those cameras installed on the drive. At least that will place him here."

"No point in pressing charges, really. You know that. I'm just glad I had my trusty little sidekick with me." She ruffled the dog's fur, careful not to hit his wounds, though they seemed to be healing at an alarming rate. She thought it must have been the good food and sleep he was getting.

"Okay then, Jo, call me direct if you see him again. If it happens again, I will be the one to file charges. I'll keep you out of it. Your daddy took care of me and mine when needed. It's time I repaid that." He tipped his hat at her and stepped out of the house. Jo watched him walk to the old cruiser he still drove, then gently closed the door. She rested her head on the cool wood for just a moment before turning to get dinner heated up. The cows would not understand if she were late with the feed, and she was pretty sure she needed to eat as well if she wanted to make it through the evening chores. Buddy lay quietly under the table, only his eyes moving, tracking her movements as she fumbled through the kitchen.

"Damn, this is going to hurt more in the morning. Not sure there's enough ibuprofen in the world to help."

Jo dragged herself through the evening routine, making sure to count cows as she went. No telling what those city folks might have done. She was sure a gate meant nothing to them. Jo hobbled back to the house and climbed in a steaming hot shower, her ribs now a shade of blue she had only seen in the night sky. She threw on her most comfortable oversized t-shirt, some clean panties, and some warm socks she knew would get kicked off in the night and crawled into bed. She never heard the coyotes singing in the night or the sound of a large dog fighting off the pack. Her night was dreamless.

Chapter 8
The Mighty Hunter?

Morning broke with an overcast sky and the threat of rain. Jo felt each and every hit she took the day before; she pushed herself into a sitting position with a groan. She did not think there were enough painkillers in the world to get her through this day or enough coffee, but she could already hear the cows lowing and knew she needed to get moving. She had not done her last walk-through of the barn the night before and was hoping all was good.

She shuffled through, getting in her jeans and an old button-down cowboy shirt her dad had worn before he passed that was loose and comfortable. The coffee was going to have to wait as the cows seemed to be all in a tizzy.

Buddy appeared right by her side as she headed out. He had a spring in his step and seemed to be excited to see her.

"Hey, Buddy, looks like you're feeling better. I'm glad one of us is." She carefully reached down to pat the little dog, aware that each movement hurt more than the last.

She got the feed robot set up. Most of what she did was automatic in the barn. She dumped the feed into large bins that mixed it up and moved it into a large robot that then went up and down the aisles, dropping feed for all the cows. It wasn't as high-tech as she wanted; that was super expensive, but all she had to do was make sure the feed got dumped in the proper ration, and the robot was turned on. Then she walked the barn to check that all the cows had made it in last night and that there were no issues with any of them.

She patted noses and ran her hand down the backs of a few. She smiled to herself, at peace in the barn. Buddy was right beside her the whole time. She slid the large doors at the end of the barn open, not remembering closing them the night before, and peeked out at the rolling pasture. The doors were large enough that it was almost the whole side of the barn, so the view was uninterrupted. In the pasture, rather close to the barn, were three piles of bloody mess.

Jo went as fast as her aching body would let her, Buddy happily prancing around her feet. As she approached, she had to cover her nose from the stench.

"What in the holy hell!" She took another step closer as Buddy zoomed by her and sat right smack in the middle of the carnage, tongue lolling out, happy as can be. She bent down to take a peek at the mess. The realization that this was once two or three coyotes made her gasp, breathing in the noxious odor of death. She gagged and stepped back. Buddy yipped at her, still smiling.

"Did you do this, Buddy?" She was astonished at the idea of her little dog tearing apart the coyotes that were three times his size. Still, the look of pure satisfaction on his face made her consider the idea.

She closed the barn door back up, unable to dispose of the corpses at this moment. She walked back toward the house deep in thought with Buddy yipping and dancing by her side. She couldn't help but let images of her little dog attacking the coyotes run through her mind. She wasn't sure how that could have happened, but she was pretty sure he at least had a hand in it.

As she approached her front porch, she saw a man lounging in one of the big comfy chairs she had placed there. Her anxiety shot up. Who the fuck was on her porch? She stomped the rest of the way, her heart thumping in her chest.

"May I help you?" Jo managed to not sound as scared or angry as she felt.

"I've come for my dog."

Chapter 9

Ashe

Buddy ran between the two of them, yipping and barking, as happy as could be.

"What have you done to him?" The stranger stared at the little dog in horror.

"I cleaned him up. He had claw marks all over him. He was almost dead out in the middle of the field during a thunderstorm." Jo's voice was monotone. The shock of someone actually looking for the little dog left her dumbfounded.

"That's not what I mean," he growled. "How could you turn him into this, this thing?"

Buddy stopped and looked sadly at the man. He walked over to him, almost dragging his feet as he went, then rolled over so the man could pet his belly.

"Yes, yes, I know it's you. But really, Cer, what happened to you?" He reached down and rubbed the dog's belly. He smiled as the dog wiggled in absolute joy at his touch.

Standing straight, he looked at Jo, "we will be leaving now. Thank you seems to be in order. I am not sure what happened to him, but I thank you for keeping him alive, even if he is in this pathetic form."

Tears started to leak from Jo's eyes. The week could not get any worse. This was the last straw, the one that was breaking her. Buddy jumped up and ran to her, launching himself into her arms. He started to lick away all her tears and snuggle into her. She laid her head on his wiggling body and hugged him before putting him down. Buddy sat on her foot, wagging his tail and looking at the man.

"We cannot take in every stray you find, Cer. I know you like this one. Yes, yes, she did save your life. Are you saying I owe her?" The man's conversation with the little dog made Jo blink hard. It was as though the dog was answering him telepathically. "She doesn't even know who we are, who you are. Yes, I see the bruises on her, fine."

He looked up, glaring at Jo. "He says we owe you his life, and we need to help you. May I come in for a bit of tea or coffee? I promise I won't hurt you unless you want me to." The way he smiled at her made Jo really notice him for the first time. He was unbelievably handsome, with dark hair that glinted with an undertone of red when the sun hit it. The man stood about six foot two and seemed athletic but not overly muscly. His suit was custom-made and fit him like a glove in all the right places. His eyes seemed to hold a fire behind them, a literal fire. Jo shook herself as she looked into them and almost lost herself. His smile showed perfect white teeth.

"I haven't even introduced myself. My name is Ashe Beliel." He strode over to her with his hand out. Though it seemed like a casual gesture, Jo could feel the pressure build around her as he moved closer, as if the air was pushed along with him. Buddy gave a slight growl as Ashe got closer.

"Fine, Cer, I won't push." And just like that, the air was light again.

Jo stared at his hand, grunted, and walked past him. Buddy jumped up and followed her into the house. She left the door open, expecting Ashe to follow. Jo started to kettle for tea but poured herself a cup of coffee. She put out some grapes and crackers, a cup with a few different tea bags, sugar, and cream. Ashe stood in the doorway with a disgusted look on his face as he saw the cheap tea.

"I'll have coffee as well, thank you." He pulled out his own chair and sat, waiting on her to pour the coffee for him.

Jo handed him a cup and sat across the table, unsure what was happening. Buddy sat under the table, tongue lolling out, looking between her and the man sitting at her table.

"Cer says we need to negotiate your keeping him for a bit. He says a man did this to your face, that he tried to take your ranch, and that the coyotes are trying to take your cattle. Cer believes that you need help and that you deserve help." The last part was said with disdain.

Jo stared at the man, still not understanding what was happening. "I have questions. Who is Cer? Who are you? What in the actual fuck are you talking about?" As the words left her mouth, she still could not believe she had invited this man into her house, a stranger! Who knew what he was capable of?

"Cer is my dog. I believe you call him Buddy." The dog's tail began to whap on the floor, keeping rhythm to an unknown beat. Jo casually put her hand down to pat him and was rewarded with kisses all over her hand.

"I am, well, let's just say I run my own type of cooperation. I am talking about that Cer is indebted to you for saving his life. For that, we need to repay a life for a life, or in this case a ranch," he looked around the kitchen again in disgust, "for a life."

"So, the dog is talking to you? Can I call someone for you?"

Ashe sighed, "yes, the dog is talking to me, and he better talk some more so I can find out who did this to him. When I do, there will be, well, Hell to pay." He leered at his own joke. Jo realized that this was probably not a safe place for her to be and began to stand up and move around the kitchen in an attempt to get to the door without him noticing.

"No need to run. I'm everywhere."

Jo turned and ran full out at the back door smacking right into Ashe.

"Really, is this necessary? I just want to get my dog's debt taken care of." She turned on her heel and ran full out at the entry to the living room, almost knocking herself out as her head slammed into his collar bone.

"Oh dear, that had to hurt. Let me look at that."

Jo backed slowly away from him as he strolled in her direction. Her head was pounding. She felt the spot where she had hit him. A knot was forming already.

"Who the fuck are you!"

Still walking toward her in no hurry, Ashe replied, "Some call me the Prince of Darkness, but honestly, I prefer Ashe. It's so much less formal, don't you think?" Her back was against the wall as he invaded her personal space. His hand went up beside her head, taking all his weight as he leaned in, "I can make that boo-boo go away. Just give me a chance to make you feel things you've never dreamed of feeling." He moved closer so that their lips were almost touching.

Jo's pulse was racing. Her head swam at the sight of the most gorgeous man she had ever known, leaning in for a kiss. A kiss that she knew would rock her world. She mentally shook herself, knowing this was not her, not really. She never let wants get before needs, though he was making it extremely hard to decide if this was an actual need or not. She saw Buddy out of the corner of her eye, stalking them as if trying to figure out which one to protect; this shook her out of whatever spell he was casting.

"Why do they call you the *Prince* of Darkness? Why aren't you king of something? That is if you are who you say you are?"

With that, his chin hit his chest, he sighed in the most annoyed way she had ever heard anyone sigh, and the spell was broken.

"Of course, that's what you need to know. I have no answer for that." He pushed off the wall and strolled back to the kitchen table. "Since that's out of the way now, let's figure out how you can keep this dump, and I can get my dog back."

Buddy yipped in joy and jumped up in Jo's arms. She wasn't quite sure what they had gotten out of the way. Her heart was still thudding, and her legs were weak, but Jo wasn't going to let one night of passion ruin her family's work. She walked gingerly over to the coffee pot and poured a shaking cup of coffee before finally turning to face the gorgeous man she had just turned down. "Thank you."

Chapter 10
You Do Like That Word

The following day started relatively normal. The cows were fed without any more dead coyotes in the field, no one was waiting on her porch. Buddy kept her company as she hummed and worked. It wasn't until about lunchtime that the day got interesting.

Jo was in her office at the house when she heard the rumble of Kyle's car. She sighed but kept working. The numbers needed to be crunched; she needed to find a way to keep this going and hopefully not be indebted to Ashe. Yes, he said he owed her, but he made her uncomfortable, and she did not want him around any more than he had to be. Kyle began to pound on the front door, yelling her name.

"Don't worry, love, I'll get it." The sing-song voice of Ashe made her jump out of the chair so fast it crashed into the wall. It was almost like her legs had a mind of their own as she flew down the stairs trying to reach the door before he did.

She could hear him chuckle right before he opened the front door.

"Who the fuck are you!" Kyle growled.

"I've been asked that a lot this week. Ashe, and you must be the Kyle. The pleasure is mine." Ashe held his hand out to shake, but Kyle pushed right past him, looking around. His gaze lasered in on Jo, who was trying to duck into the shadows at the bottom of the stairs.

"Who the fuck is he? Did you get a new fuck buddy?"

"You do like that word a lot, don't you, Kyle." Ashe appeared right next to the other man, smiling serenely at him. "Actually, she had declined to fuck me, much to my disappointment. Though I'm pretty sure she turned you down as well. Am I right?" Ashe tilted his head to the side like he was asking an old friend for his opinion.

Jo wasn't sure her eyes could get any wider. Kyle turned on Ashe as if to strike him.

"I would rethink that if I were you, Kyle." Each time Ashe said his name, it became more and more like an insult. "I am not Jo; in fact, I am Jo's attorney. I will not sit and let you hit me, I will not stop the dog from tearing you up, and I will, in fact, press charges, after which I will sue you for everything you've got and then some."

Jo found Ashe's smile creepy. It never left his face since Kyle had arrived. Buddy launched himself from the steps, deep growls reverberating through the room. Ashe stepped forward and caught the little dog in mid-jump. "Now, now, Buddy, we will take care of him the right way. No need to get your pretty teeth all stained with blood."

With the dog tucked securely under his arm Ashe walked toward the kitchen, only pausing long enough to look over his shoulder and wink at Kyle. This set the other man in a frenzy.

"Oh, now you have a lawyer to fight me! And who the fuck is he? Do you really think you can win, Jo? I own this town." As he yelled, he moved closer to her, so the last part was said with his finger directly in her face.

Jo felt the low rumbling in the floor before she heard it. Her back was pressed against the wall leaving her with no option of escape as she saw the blur hit Kyle full force.

Buddy stood on top of him again, growling and drooling. This time Jo had no problem seeing the three-headed dog. Its fur was a dark grey, almost black. The shape of his head was more of a bully breed than that of the little terrier Jo knew. He had tripled in size, the muscles rippling under his fur.

"Cerberus is not a fan of you, Kyle. He takes his guarding role very seriously. Right now, he wishes to guard Jo. So next time you come, maybe just think about that before rushing in to threaten her." Ashe was leaning nonchalantly on the door frame; Jo made a mental note that he seemed to do this a lot. "Cer, come." The dog didn't budge. Drool was hitting Kyle in the face. "Jo, I think he's waiting on you to call him off. He's your guard now, not mine." Ashe smiled wickedly at her.

"Umm, Cer? Buddy? Come." In a blink of an eye, her Buddy was right back at her side. Brown and white tail flapping on the floor, long terrier nose sporting a smile from ear to ear. Jo patted his head and whispered that he was a good dog, then turned back to Kyle, who was dragging himself up from the floor.

"You are not allowed within one hundred feet of me. That will be legal tomorrow after I see the judge. You are not allowed on my property again; I will have you arrested for trespass. And if you think you can scare me into turning over my family's land, you obviously don't know me very well. Get out."

She turned back toward the kitchen, winking at Ashe as she passed him.

Chapter 11
The Most Inane Questions

Jo was setting the coffee pot up when Ashe wandered back into the room. "He's gone. What an ass! No wonder Cer doesn't want to leave you here."

She smiled at his comment. Seriously, if the Prince of Darkness is calling you an ass, you might have a problem. She started to giggle uncontrollably. Buddy looked up at her, tongue lolling out, a big smile on his face. She crumbled to the floor, still laughing, to hold on to the little dog. How her life was headed just left her no room but to laugh. Her stability was a small dog that was masquerading his true three-headed self while demanding that the Devil himself do her bidding.

Tears started to leak from her eyes as the laughter continued to roll. Buddy licked the tears off her cheeks and snuggled into her arms, sharing his warmth with her.

"This really isn't the time." Ashe was exasperated with her nonsense which really made her laugh harder.

"Ashe, how did you get into the house to let him in? You left last night; I am sure of it." She wiped the tears away and smiled at her little Buddy. "Not that I'm mad you got to meet him, but how did you get here?"

"And again, this is what you ask? You ask the most inane questions. I am the Prince of Darkness. I come and go as I please. Is that enough of an answer? Please come and see the plan I've devised to keep your ranch. I am ready to be done with this and to go home with my dog."

Jo gathered herself together, grabbed two cups of coffee, and sat at the table, trying to keep enough space between Ashe and herself so she would not get distracted.

"I won't bite unless you want me to." His smile was like fire. Jo caught her breath and was mesmerized until Buddy let out a low growl.

"Fine! You used to be fun, dog." Ashe turned back to the computer, releasing Jo from his hold on her. She sighed with relief and mentally promised Buddy a big steak for dinner.

"So, from what I see on the records, you do owe a bit of money. But I am also seeing that it's in a freeze, so nothing should be charged at the moment. That said, it will not tell me a total, nor will it let me pay for the fees. Really this should be an easy fix. Nothing needed from me other than some cash. Is that right?"

"Umm, yes? I'm not sure how much the total is, so I might actually have the money, but they keep charging fees for being the executor of dads will. They also will not release any of the money or the title left to me because they say I owe back taxes or something. I can't get a straight answer is the main issue. That and Kyle will keep it hanging and charging me until he knows I can't pay, or I give up." Jo sat dejectedly, staring at the laptop screen. She had gone over all the numbers that were there hundreds of times. Nothing seemed out of the ordinary. It all appeared on the up and up until you got to the part where Kyle was still charging her and not releasing the money or land. Any payments she made to him were set aside in a separate account, not put towards the amount owed. So she could pay and pay, but it never made the numbers go down.

"Hmmm, okay. This seems easy enough. Just leave it to me." With that, Ashe closed the laptop gently, patted Buddy on the head, then patted Jo on the head and walked out.

Jo sat there for a moment; her head was warm where he had touched her. She shook herself, wondering if she was in the same realm as the dog was to him. "Well, it's not like you're a beauty queen or anything. You probably smell like cow poop." Buddy whined gently and laid his head on her foot, gazing at her with such adoration that she felt terrible about getting down on herself.

"You love me and want to be with me. That's what matters. Thanks, Buddy. Love you too." She squished the little dog's face in her hands and then headed out with him on her heels to check on the cattle.

Chapter 12
Lots of People Don't Like Me

The Sheriff pulled into the long drive just as she was finishing up the morning chores the next day. He parked and gently closed the cruiser door. Looking at her, he took his hat off and held it in front of his chest. Even though she wasn't close enough to him to see his expression, she could tell by his body language that something was wrong.

She hustled up to the front of the house, only stopping long enough to close the barn door and make sure buddy was by her side.

"Sheriff, how can I help you this morning?"

"Well, Jo, I was wondering if Kyle had come up here last night?"

"He was up here yesterday, but he left before supper. Is everything alright?"

"He's in real bad shape today. Someone found him lying on the side of the road right by your drive about three this morning. I've been trying to track his movements. I know we talked about him coming up here and that you should call me first, but I don't know. I thought maybe he came up, and you had had enough and beat the snot outta him."

"No, sir, I hadn't seen him since supper. He did leave in a tizzy, though. He was mad I got a lawyer to fight him to keep the ranch. He said some not-nice things and then stormed out of the house. That was the last I saw him."

"Lawyer, eh? Good on you, girl! Was the lawyer here when he was here?"

"Yep, he was. But we sat for about two or three hours working through paperwork for the court case. I doubt it could be him." She hoped her face did not betray the fact that she was reasonably sure Ashe had beat the snot out of Kyle last night.

"Okay, then, Jo, let me know if you hear anything." He climbed back in his cruiser, and Jo watched him pull back down the driveway.

"He deserved it, you know." She knew he would be there, so the sound of his voice did not startle her. Jo thought maybe she was getting better at this working with the Devil thing. Standing on her porch in a pair of snug-fitting wranglers and a pearl button, off-white shirt, he could have been an ad for a dirty cowboy movie. His skin was just tan enough to look like he worked in the sun, making Jo wonder if Hell gave off UV rays.

Her face must have shown her thought process a little; Ashe sighed and headed inside, where he poured her a glass of sweet tea.

"You do know sweet tea is a southern thing, not really a ranch thing."

He stopped pouring and looked a little startled, "Oh, I just thought it was a rural thing. Good to know. Do you still want it? I can make something else."

"No, the tea is fine, thank you. You could have left him anyplace. Why would you bring him back to my drive?"

"Well, that's the thing, I didn't. I would never have tried to bring attention to you. The point of this was to get him to leave you alone, not to bother you more."

They sat at the kitchen table, Buddy thumping his tail on the floor below, staring at each of them in turn, both at a loss as to how Kyle had gotten to Jo's drive.

"Did he have his car when you saw him?"

"He was at his house. He didn't know it was me. I can take on any size and shape." He looked pointedly at her, but Jo chose to ignore his hint.

"So, someone else doesn't like him as much as I don't. Maybe someone who is also being ripped off by him."

"But Jo, he was dropped here. To make you look bad. That sounds like they don't like you either."

Jo waved the idea off, "I'm a female rancher. Lots of people don't like me. But what if they wanted me to find him? What if they think I am in bed with him?" She shuddered at the thought.

"Ooohh, maybe. I'll go see what I can find out. Stay safe." He stood and planted a kiss right on the top of her head, shooting heat straight to her toes. Buddy let out a soft grown and jumped into her lap as if claiming her before Ashe could.

His deep chuckle bounced around the front hall as he left.

Chapter 13
Ashe not Ass

The day had been long but good. Jo had worked the ranch all day. All the heifers and steer were sorted and accounted for, the chicken coop was cleaned, the vegetable garden was weeded, and the hay field was almost ready for the second cut. In all, it was a satisfying day, especially with Buddy by her side. Whenever she got too serious, he would do something silly to make her laugh or just lay his head on her foot while she drove the tractor. These were the days that made ranching worth it.

She was exhausted but in a good way. She ate some leftovers, took a boiling hot shower, threw on an oversized t-shirt, and crawled into bed, looking forward to the next day. She felt her hair moving across her face, but it didn't wake her up entirely. It just made her roll over so the ceiling fan would stop blowing on her.

Her hair continued to tickle her face, then the mattress began to vibrate. The movement that finally shot her out of sleep was the launching of a four-legged beast across her as it hit a person dead in the chest, knocking him into the wall. She knew it was him by the deep grunt he let out.

Jo jumped what felt like ten feet in the other direction as Buddy/Cerberus had a body pinned between the wall and the floor. She was reaching for the gun when the fact that the man was laughing made her stop in her tracks. "You ass!"

"Ashe, not ass." He flipped the giant three-headed dog on its back and began giving it belly rubs. Cerberus wiggled in joy, grunting and whining as Ashe joyfully gave a full round of pets to his dog. Kneeling on the floor with Cer, Ashe looked up at Jo, "so, I've done some snooping about, and I believe we might have more of an issue than originally thought. I think I figured out who tried to destroy Cer, which leads directly into who is trying to destroy you."

Jo froze. She hadn't really thought of it as someone trying to destroy her before. She mulled this over for a few seconds, then, in the honest fashion of her family, pushed it aside so she could concentrate on what Ashe was saying. Cerberus had not changed back to his Buddy form, but that wiggly body and drooly tongue hanging out while Ashe crawled on the floor with him made her smile. He may not look like her little friend, but he still acted the same.

Jo stepped back to the bed and grabbed a pillow to hang onto. Lost in thought, she did not notice that the playing had stopped.

"Jo, maybe you should put some pants on unless you want to take more off." She shook herself out of her reverie and jumped to grab the grey sweats hung on the back of her chair. She always kept some close in case she needed to run out to the barn at night. Turning back, she saw her little Buddy was back to his smaller self.

"That better?" she asked sarcastically, modeling her oversized sweats to match her oversized shirt.

Ashe laughed a little and nodded. "Let's head down and get some coffee. This may take a while to explain. You too, Cer. You need to hear this as well."

Jo wondered what could be going on as Ashe moved with a purpose around the kitchen. He started the coffee, reached into the fridge, grabbed some eggs, ham, and cheese, and started to whip together an omelet. The smell was divine, like nothing she had ever smelled before, which she found odd since she had watched him and knew he hadn't even added salt.

He poured her a cup, mixing in the half and half and sugar precisely the way she liked it, and brought the cup and an omelet over, placing them in front of her. Jo closed her eyes and breathed in the tantalizing scent; the smile Ashe gave her when she opened her eyes could have melted plastic.

"I can make this for you anytime you want, Jo." He waggled his eyebrows at her ruining the look. She chuckled and dug into the eggs, groaning in ecstasy after the first bite.

"Okay, now that you've buttered me up with amazing food and coffee, which by the way, thank you for knowing how I take it, can you tell me why you woke me up in the middle of the night?"

Ashe sat and fiddled with his shirt, ensuring the collar was just right. Jo realized he was nervous, which made her nervous. Seriously who or what could possibly make the Prince of Darkness nervous.

"So, um, we have a minor issue with the whole Kyle thing. First off, it was a setup. Him being dumped here. It just wasn't a very good one. This brings us to the other issue. Who tried to destroy Cerberus? There are very few things in this or any other realm that can do damage to him like that. Mostly powerful beings such as myself, that's about it. And I didn't do it to him." Buddy/Cer nuzzled Ashe's hand, letting him know Cer knew it wasn't Ashe that had harmed him.

"Okay, so then who, or what, are we dealing with?" The idea of a being as powerful or more so than Ashe made her uncomfortable. And why would they be going after her?

"Belphegor." Jo stared at Ashe, unable to understand what he was saying.

"Excuse me? Who or what is Belphegor?"

Ashe sighed long and deep, "one of the fallen, like myself. Only he was tossed out for not caring. He chose neither God's side in the argument nor mine, so he was tossed out, never to be welcomed anywhere. He came to earth and lived many lives here, always trying to create his own kingdom. He has done things that were blamed on me. Hitler was one of his manifestations, as well as things credited to God. He has been more than one Pope throughout the ages. I'm not quite sure what he wants now. But I do believe he is Kyle's lawyer."

Jo sat in silence, digesting what Ashe had just said. "Wait, I thought all those tossed from Heaven were yours to rule. That's kinda what they teach in Sunday school."

"I know! All but Bel. He never did care for authority." He said this with such despair that Jo had to laugh. Here he was, the Devil himself, frustrated with someone's lack of heeding authority. It just struck her as funny until she looked down to where the marks still shown faintly on Buddy.

"I'll kill him myself for what he did to Buddy!" The rage overtook her so quickly that she threw the chair back and started to march out the door. Buddy ran to get between her and the door, but she moved past him. He ran ahead again, but this time in the form of the three-headed guardian of Hell. His growl shook the walls as he stood, blocking her only way out. It gave Ashe enough time to catch up. He swung Jo around to face him. Her eyes still burned with fury; Ashe did the only thing he could think of to drown the anger. He kissed her. He kissed her with such heat as if to suck the anger right out of her.

Slowly Jo could feel his fingers digging into her shoulders. She opened her eyes to see his staring right back. She lifted her hands as if to caress his chest, then pushed him away. She stumbled backward, tripping over the dog and landing right smack on her behind. Cerberus did not mind her being at his level and proceeded to slobber all over her.

"Sorry, luv, I didn't know any other way. Does that happen often? Or is it just me?" His smile usually warmed her to her toes, but it left her ice-cold this time. She had never lost her cool like that before. It left her shaking to realize how close she was to marching out the door.

"Umm, no. That's a first." She kept her eyes down. She could not look at him.

"Okay," he blew out a breath and ran his hand through his hair. "This might be an issue then, but it could just be suppressed emotion that finally had to be released. We are going to think it's that, alright? I mean, really, Jo, you have been dealing with a lot. This might have just been the last straw. Two fallen angels, one super sexy and one, well, one unpredictable one. It would lead lesser men to break. We will just keep an eye on you." Jo just nodded and wrapped her arms around the big dog.

She felt Cerberus shift just a bit. There, extended out was Ashe's hand to help her up. She took it, still slightly embarrassed by her outburst. He didn't seem to mind; he hoisted her to her feet and led her back to the kitchen.

"Well, there's not much to do but wait for the next thing, I guess." He smiled at her sadly. "I am sorry you are somehow in all of this. Cer and I are grateful that you were out in the shitty weather trying to catch some shitty cows that night. Without you, who knows what would have happened to him." Cer laid his head on Ashe's knee but thunked his tail on Jo's leg. The dog seemed to be totally content between the two people he loved best.

Chapter 14
A Delivery

The chores started very early, especially after such a late night. Jo left Ashe in the kitchen on the computer, working on the case, she guessed. Buddy tagged along with her as she hauled feed and hay, checked on calves, checked the fence line close to the house, and noted that she would have to schedule a day to head out to check the fence line. Maybe she could get a neighbor kid to come with her as an extra set of hands to make the fence repair go quicker. She was lost in thought as she brought the all-terrain vehicle back to the barn. She almost didn't see the beat-up old car struggling down the drive. Buddy alerted her to the intruder with a low growl.

Jo didn't hurry. She put the vehicle up, stepped out, wiped off her pants, sighed, and headed out to see if the car had yet made it to the house. It had, but with such a commotion, Ashe had actually stepped out on the porch to see what it was. As she approached them from the side, their view of her was obscured by the house. She could see the disheveled younger man try to hand Ashe a manila folder, then snatch it back as if he had been burned. Ashe's smile looked sinister.

"If you are not the recipient, then I cannot hand it to you! It needs to go to this lady and only her."

Jo stepped around the corner and stopped. "I'm Josephine if that's who you are looking for." The young man turned toward her, and his whole body relaxed as if the sight of Ashe brought tension to him. Jo looked at Ashe, who just shrugged his shoulders as if he hadn't done anything, and went back into the house.

She took the folder and instructed the young man that if he drove on the grass by the side of the drive, he might have better luck getting out since it wouldn't be as full of ruts or mud. He thanked her and almost ran to his car.

"What's that?" Ashe's voice startled her. "I would assume it's some type of legal form since he wouldn't give it to me, no matter how much I tried to persuade him." Again, with that heart-stopping grin. Jo just grunted and pushed past him into the house.

"You know, if you can't persuade a simple delivery boy to hand you an envelope, I'm not sure how much confidence I have in your being my lawyer."

Ashe pretended to be offended but just chuckled. "I wasn't trying too hard. I knew you were around the corner. Besides, he plays hard for the other side. They are often more difficult to sway. No worries, once we are in court, none of them is extreme in their faith."

While speaking, Ashe took the folder out of Jo's hands and opened it. "Ooohhh, so they are pushing for a foreclosure. I think we will file a countersuit of fraud and theft. Now the fun will begin!" He turned back to his computer, gathered it all up, kissed Jo on the forehead, and left without another word.

"Well, Buddy, let's hope he can do what he says, or we are screwed." Jo sat hard in the kitchen chair. Buddy, her ever-present cheerleader, laid his head on her lap and thumped his tail on the floor.

Chapter 15
Court

The months waiting for the court date had been Hell, though Ashe would disagree. He thought it had been fun to go back and forth with Bel and Kyle. They wanted to foreclose, and he sued them. They wanted payment now. He sued them. They wanted to make a deal, and he sued them. Each time he submitted a suit he cackled with delight.

While this went on, the ranch barely made enough money to stay afloat. At no point did Kyle ever say he would release her inheritance. That was never something that was discussed. Ashe ensured Jo had anything she needed, but she did her best to not need a single thing. The idea of possibly owing a favor to this man, demon, or whatever he was, did not sit well with her. She tried her best to do it all herself. With her little Buddy by her side, it seemed as though she could. Surprisingly, Ashe didn't try to get in her pants once while they waited. He stayed at her house mostly but seemed to always find other places to be. If she was in the kitchen, he was in the living room. If she was on the porch, he was on the back patio. If she hadn't been so worried about the upcoming battle, she might have been offended slightly, though relieved at the same time. As it was, the idea that he was avoiding her was a passing thought most days, nothing to stand out.

The day of the court hearing dawned chilly and bright. Fall was in the air. Jo could think of a million things that needed to get done before the snows came. She sighed at the idea of having to spend so much of her precious time fighting for what was rightfully hers. As they entered the courthouse, Ashe reached over and rubbed her back a bit.

"It will be over soon, and honestly, I have never lost a case." Jo had to chuckle a bit at this. She did have the advantage of having the Devil himself as her counsel. She saw Kyle and Bel in the hallway. This was the first time she had laid eyes on the other fallen angel. She had thought he would be as handsome and charming as Ashe, but he seemed to resemble a weasel. He was short and thin; his back was somewhat bent, making him appear as though he led everything with his prominent nose. Jo just stared for a moment.

"Yes, not what you would expect. But remember, luv, we can change our appearance to fit whatever our needs are. From this look and the back and forth we just went through, I would say he is here to cause havoc, and that is all. He wants to revel in the chaos of what he has done. Don't let the outside fool you, though. He's sneaky as a, well, weasel." He smiled and winked at her, then ushered her into the courtroom.

Kyle came in right behind them, running smack into her. Jo's stumble was caught with one hand by Ashe. He set her right, then turned to Bel, "Control your client, Bel. I will file harassment and assault charges."

Bel snorted, "Like she has any room to talk with that little incident of beating him within an inch of his life." Ashe let out a spontaneous laugh making both other men step back.

"We both know that wasn't Jo. There is no way that she could have done any of that damage after the beating she took a few days before. It is funny how he somehow got to the top of her drive, though. As if it was a plant of sorts. If you pursue the idea that it was Jo, we will bring out the truth, and neither of you wants that, now do you?" He stared intently at Kyle, who wilted under the gaze. They all moved towards their respective places, Kyle side eying Jo whenever he thought she wasn't looking. Jo ignored him even though she wanted to go punch him in his face and demand he set this all right. She glanced at Ashe, who was busy setting up his computer and organizing his papers. She knew she was going to win. At least she had a pretty good idea she might, with Ashe at the helm.

She took a moment to look at her surroundings. The courtroom looked similar to those Jo saw on tv, nothing fancy and a lot smaller than she thought it would be. She was nervous and wished Buddy could be there with her. She smirked at the thought of how he could take Kyle down even though he really didn't look like much, just a small, beat-up dog. She sobered with a glance at Bel and Kyle's table. That was what Bel was doing. The weasel-looking man glanced at her and smiled, knowing she was thinking of the little dog.

Her anger bubbled up again, and Bel's smile just got bigger. Ashe gently placed a hand on her thigh, heat shooting up from the spot knocking the anger right out of her, replaced with other things.

"Remember, he answers to no one, makes his own rules, and enjoys chaos. He is pulling on your ever-so-visible strings to get you riled up. Take a breath and let it go. Each time you feel the anger take a deep breath and let it go. Imagine the anger leaving your body. Imagine a calm setting over you. You need to control this."

Jo closed her eyes and did as she was told. Not only did it shake off the last remnants of the anger, but it also shook off the heat from Ashe's hand. She was happy to see that she could be in control no matter which one of the fallen was trying to pull her strings.

The court got called to order, and the proceedings began. It was rather dull for the most part. This was not a jury trial. There was just the judge who would rule on the outcome. The beginning was just presenting evidence without calling any actual witnesses. Jo couldn't believe there would be any actual people who could or would testify for or against her. No one really knew the ins and outs of what was happening except Kyle, who knew it too well. He was using his influence and obscure legalities to keep her from moving forward with the ranch.

Bel would make a point; Ashe would counter it. Back and forth for what felt like an eternity. Bel produced the back amount owed to Kyle, Ashe produced the records of payments made held in an account and never credited. Bel came back with a point about death taxes. Ashe returned to the records and proof that the will had never been executed and Jo had never received the life insurance payouts or the titles to the land and property.

It seemed rather boring and straightforward. Even the judge was getting annoyed at Kyle and Bel for not allowing her to move forward, or at least that was Jo's impression.

Jo started to pay more attention when the judge called for witnesses to be called. She glanced at Ashe, who deliberately did not look at her.

Bel called Kyle to the stand.

Jo sat up a little straighter and took a deep breath.

Bel stood up and smirked at the room.

Ashe sat in stony silence.

"Mr. Brown, good morning. Can you explain to the court why you are bringing this case?"

Kyle put on a sad face, turned to the judge, and began his sob story about how he and his family had taken care of the legal issues of the ranch for Jo's dad and about how they had always been there for Jo's family. That it wasn't really something he wanted to do, but, alas, he needed to get paid so that he would not lose his own home. If Jo would just pay her debts, he would gladly release the inheritance, or if she couldn't, if she would just let him sell the ranch so they could both make a little money.

Jo had a hard time not rolling her eyes. She behaved and glared at Kyle as he spoke.

Bel finished up with Kyle, letting Ashe see a smirk as he walked back to the table. Ashe stood, straightened his suit jacket, unbuttoned the jacket's top button, and strode to the podium.

"Isn't it true, Mr. Brown, that you have your sights set on the land that my client's ranch is on to make into a luxury resort?"

Without hesitation, Kyle looked appalled while replying, "No, I would never do that! I just want Jo to keep her family ranch. I am doing everything I can. I just need her to pay her debts."

"I would like to refer to plaintiff evidence number 163. If you look at it, you will see where my client has made payments to you, and you have put them all in a holding account without applying the amount toward the debt. Not only that, but you then continue to charge exorbitant interest on the original debt while increasing the amount owed each time the interest is added, isn't that correct?"

"Yes, sir, legally, without it being paid in full, I do not have to apply that amount."

Ashe smiled slightly, "where, Mr. Brown, does it say this on the contract. Which by the way, where is my client's signature on the contract? Or, for that matter, where is the contract?"

Kyle innocently as he could replied, "I am the family attorney. I had her father's signature. I do not need hers."

"So, what you are saying, Mr. Brown, is that you have no contract with my client."

Kyle stuttered on the stand. Ashe turned on his heel, thanked Kyle for his time, and dismissed him.

Bel stood abruptly, tossing the table across the room and snapping his fingers, his face contorting into that of a beast. There was no hiding who he was at this moment. He was one of the fallen. Jo watched as Kyle froze in mid-stand; the judge and bailiff both froze in mid-yell. Bel snarled as he turned toward Ashe.

"Must you always win! Must I always come in behind you!"

Under the table, Ashe tapped Jo's foot with his before standing up, acknowledging that he knew she was not affected by whatever spell Bel had placed on the courtroom.

"I'm not really sure what to tell you, Bel. I am the Prince of Darkness, after all. And you, you are an afterthought. Well, that's not entirely true, you were given a chance to be a warrior for either side, but you decided not to. You have shown repeatedly that you have no real conviction either way. Not good, not evil. Just, well, there."

Bel flew through the air at Ashe, who easily sidestepped the attack. "Really, Bel, do you think you can get one over on me? I have had centuries of attacks to ward off from much better opponents than you could ever wish to be. There is nothing that you could do that would be surprising or new. Leave off now. Let us be done with this realm and let these mortals continue on with their rather boring lives." Ashe glanced at his fingernails as if assessing how long the manicure would take to correct all the damage the human world had done to them.

"There is one trick I have, Ashe, your little dog. I hurt him. Cerberus is not immortal like you; I will make him bleed!"

Jo's anger began as a slow burn. Bel still had not realized she was not frozen in place as he continued with his tirade.

"He healed because of her, but he won't be so lucky next time. I'll make sure to dump him where the lesser demons can devour him." He did not see it coming when Jo slapped the grin off his face.

She had never been so angry before, her Buddy. He was threatening her Buddy! How dare he think he could get away with that. Bel stood, shook off the shock, and came at her with his fingers bared as if they were claws. She swatted him away like he was a fly landing on one of her cows. The growls reverberated through the room. Jo thought it was Ashe until the grey streak landed on Bel, tearing his cheek off and leaving a glittering bloody mess, then bolting back to Jo.

Cerberus had learned a few things from his last battle with the demon. His body filled the space so that both Jo and Ashe were cornered with little room to move around in. Cer circled Bel, ignoring Ashe and Jo. As the three-headed dog launched, Bel stood, ready for attack. He laughed and launched himself at the dog. Cer saw it coming and tore a piece of his forearm off.

Jo watched the battle through an orange haze. Her anger never subsided, just increasing with the worry about her little dog, who didn't seem so little or helpless right now.

Bel reached into his coat, withdrew a long katana, and squared off with Cer. The three-headed dog continued to circle him, each head growling and keeping eyes on him. In a flash, Bel was on him. Jo hadn't even seen the demon move. She just heard the yelp from Cer, then watched as the dog's image flickered between the three-headed monster and her little Buddy. Blood was pouring out of a gash that scored the entire length of the dog's back.

Jo didn't feel herself move until she had grabbed the sword from Bel's hand. With a snarl she didn't recognize, she thrust the blade into the demon's gut. With both hands she pushed the knife up through his ribcage and into where his heart should have been. The demon's look of surprise was the last thing she saw as he melted into dust.

As the last of him faded, the courtroom came alive again, just for a split second before Ashe froze time.

"Well, love, it seems we have some chatting to do once we get out of here." He gently laid his suit jacket on the little dog and lifted him. Buddy let out a heart-wrenching whimper before going limp in Ashe's arms.

As he started to walk away, Jo turned to the frozen courtroom, "what about them, and what about my ranch? We can't just leave them here?"

Ashe chuckled, "No problem, luv, I've got it handled. They will wake up in their homes with the memory of Kyle losing the case, you get the ranch, and no one will be the wiser."

The anger that had taken over Jo bubbled to the surface once again, "You mean to tell me that you could have solved this months ago?"

He paused and glanced over his shoulder at her, "yes and no. Jo, I had to find out who did this to Cer. The only way was to keep working on your ranch issue until someone stepped forward. So yes, I could have solved the ranch thing, but then, you would have been indebted to me. Now you have helped me solve the Cerberus thing, and I have helped you with the ranch thing. All a wash, no debts to anyone." He smiled that smile that, at one time, made butterflies dance in her stomach. Now she just saw him for what he was. A schemer who could have taken advantage of her but chose to save his dog instead.

She sighed and followed him out of the courthouse.

Chapter 16
The Winner

The shivering would not stop. Jo wasn't really cold, but somehow her core felt freezing all at the same time. She couldn't hold the cup of coffee that Ashe tried to hand her. It sloshed over the side. He tried to put a blanket on her, but then she felt as though she were burning up. Buddy sat on her feet, trying his best to calm her.

"You won. The ranch is yours. The money is yours. Of course, that's not what we really need to discuss. Jo, tell me about your family tree. Tell me about this land. How long has your family had it?"

Jo couldn't stop her teeth from chattering as she thought back on what she knew. Everything related to the ranch, she knew it had been in the family for generations. She also knew it was almost lost during the great depression after her great grandfather died. She had always heard tales of how her grandmother had held it all together, feeding and caring for six children while keeping the ranch running. If Jo thought it was a man's world now, she could not imagine what life must have been like for a single mom fighting to keep her world together. There had been rumors, of course, of her great grandmother selling off her children. Mostly of how she sold her oldest daughter to some men, but none of that could be proven in any way. Records were scarce, if there were any at all.

Ashe blinked slowly. "How did your family keep the ranch, Jo? This isn't the first time someone has tried to take it. I thought it looked familiar, but so much has changed over time."

"My Grandmother, June, kept the ranch."

His laugh was intoxicating, low and deep. The walls seemed to bounce the joy back at them. "Well, love, I have good and bad news, and it's all the same." The smile that once lit fires in her belly now was just a smile to her. He put his hand on her leg to stop the shivering, but no heat rose.

"You, my love, are part demon. In fact, you are part of the royalty of Hell." He laughed at her shocked face. "It makes sense, really. I never could seduce you. You are the child of the bastard son I created with your grandma June."

"No, she had six kids with my grandfather. Before he died."

"Check the dates, luv. That last one was in no way your grandfather's brat. I believe she called him Robert, but I didn't really care all that much. She made a deal with the Devil to keep the ranch. A very binding deal, it seems. It seems as though I am to always make sure this land stays in your family. Though now that we know the truth, you should be able to handle yourself, don't you agree, granddaughter? Now, you need to keep a check on that temper, or bad things might begin to happen. I could show you how to do that, and I might come back to do just that at some point, but for now, I am ready to go home. Well, nothing more for me here. Come Cer."

But the dog did not move.

Louder this time, "Cerberus, come, it's time we went back to guarding the gates of hell."

Again the dog didn't even lift his head.

Ashe roared, "I said come!"

Buddy flickered, and there, laying at Jo's feet, was the three-headed beast, the guardian of Hell, the terror of the sinful. He thumped his gigantic tail on the floor but did not move one inch.

Jo reached down and patted him on the head closest to her.

"It seems as though the gates of Hell begin here, Ashe. He stays with me." She felt the heat rise in her. She threw the blanket off and stood eye to eye with the Prince of Darkness as the air rushed around her lifting her hair as if it had a life of its own. Her vision had a tint of orange to it. She had never felt so powerful and free in her entire life.

"My dog." The sound echoed through the house as if running from room to room to let all know that Cerberus was to stay there.

They stared each other down for what felt like an eternity before Ashe turned on his heel. "Well, luv, you are mostly mortal after all. At some point, you will die, then I will get my dog back. I have eternity to wait." With that, a black mist surrounded Jo and Cer; when it cleared, Ashe was gone, and Buddy stood in the spot the three-headed dog had just been.

Jo patted him on his head, sighed, and headed out to check the cows.

Don't miss out!

Visit the website below and you can sign up to receive emails whenever Terry Hooker publishes a new book. There's no charge and no obligation.

https://books2read.com/r/B-A-NSGX-TBGHC

Connecting independent readers to independent writers.

Did you love *Dog Days*? Then you should read *Ides of May*[1] by Terry Hooker!

[2]

How do you become a demon you ask? Well let me tell you our story.

In the time of the Great Depression, money and morals were in short supply. The selling of children was not unheard of. Annick's mother thought more of the mighty dollar than her own daughter, never questioning what was to become of her. Little did she know the power she was to allow her daughter to become!

That was how she met me, and how we become we.

---

1. https://books2read.com/u/bQN1zE

2. https://books2read.com/u/bQN1zE

I am the mighty Maymon, Demon King of the South! All powerful in the underneath, but until summoned, barred from walking in the sunshine of the above. Annick was chosen for me, hand picked by those who meant to control us. Lucky for me, and the girl, she had other ideas.

What a magnificent team we are! Come, hear our story. Then maybe you too could become a demon!

Also by Terry Hooker

Devil's Land Stories
Ides of May
Dog Days

About the Author

About the Author: Terry Hooker is a bestselling author, freelance writer and editor, a Jersey girl from the shore turned Florida farm girl. She has a BA in anthropology, an AAS in Culinary Arts, and an MA in Library science. She has worked as a congressional archivist, historian, teacher, and professional chef and has presented her research on the history and iconography of southern cemeteries throughout the Southeast United States. She has edited several children's books, full length novels, dissertations, and academic papers; Terry, herself, has published scholarly papers, magazine articles, fictional stories, and books. She lives with her husband, two kids, and a plethora of critters.

You can follow her on Instagram: https://www.instagram.com/thooker_author or facebook: https://www.facebook.com/Terry-Hooker-Author